DON'T BE AFRAID, AMANDA

BOOKS BY LILIAN MOORE

Papa Albert

I Feel the Same Way

I Thought I Heard the City

Sam's Place

See My Lovely Poison Ivy

To See the World Afresh
(COMPILED BY LILIAN MOORE AND
JUDITH THURMAN)

Think of Shadows

Something New Begins . . .

I'll Meet You at the Cucumbers

Don't Be Afraid, Amanda

Lilian Moore

DON'T BE AFRAID, AMANDA

Illustrated by Kathleen Garry McCord

A Jean Karl Book
Atheneum   1992   New York
Maxwell Macmillian Canada
Toronto
Maxwell Macmillan International
New York   Oxford   Singapore   Sydney

Atheneum
Macmillan Publishing Company
866 Third Avenue
New York, NY 10022

Maxwell Macmillan Canada, Inc.
1200 Eglinton Avenue East
Suite 200
Don Mills, Ontario M3C 3N1

Macmillan Publishing Company is part of the Maxwell Communication
Group of Companies.

First edition
Printed in the United States of America
10 9 8 7 6 5 4 3 2 1
The text of this book is set in 14 pt. Bembo.
Book design by Tania García

Library of Congress Cataloging-in-Publication Data

Moore, Lilian.
Don't be afraid, Amanda/Lilian Moore.—1st ed.
p.   cm.
"A Jean Karl book."
Summary: Having entertained her country pen pal Adam in the city, town
mouse Amanda overcomes her fear of the country to visit him among the
pleasures and dangers of nature. Sequel to "I'll Meet You at the
Cucumbers."
ISBN 0-689-31725-5
[1. Mice—Fiction.   2. Country life—Fiction.   3. Friendship—Fiction.]
I. Title.
PZ7.M7865Do 1992
[Fic]—dc20   91–19661

For Sam, of course
—L.M.
To Telina and Carly
—K.G.M.

WHAT WENT BEFORE

In the book *I'll Meet You at the Cucumbers,*
Adam Mouse, a shy country fellow, overcomes his fear of the city and goes with his
friend Junius, a great traveler, to meet his
pen friend, Amanda Mouse. Among his ad-
ventures in the city is a trip to the library
with his friend Amanda, where he discovers
that he is a poet. Amanda fears the country
as much as Adam has feared the city but
indicates, when asked, that, yes, she might
come someday to visit him.

CHAPTER 1

Adam Mouse was feeling nervous. His mind was full of questions. Was Amanda Mouse really coming to the country? Would she really be on the farmer's truck? Why was the truck taking so long?

Adam sighed deeply and said aloud,

> "*Waiting*
> *is a road that*
> *winds*
>
> *winds to a faraway*
> *end.*

No matter how you
hurry
the road has another bend."

"Thinking again, eh, Adam?" Chipmunk
called from a branch of the apple tree. "Can't
be good for your brain, all that thinking. What is it? What's this about waiting?"

Chipmunk was the last one Adam
wanted to talk to right now, Chipmunk so
greedy to know everything that was going on.

But he replied politely, "I'm waiting for
a friend who may be coming from the city."

"Is that so?" cried Chipmunk. "From
the city! Is that so! Do you want me to help
you wait?"

"No, thank you," said Adam quickly.
He excused himself and ran off to the garden. When he was worried, he always found
it helpful to munch on some crisp vegetable.

Crunching on a small sweet carrot,
Adam went back to the thinking that Chipmunk had interrupted.

Everything seemed to have happened so
quickly. First, the farmer had started going
to the city once and even twice a day to get

his corn to the Farmer's Market while it was still fresh.

Junius Mouse, of course, would never miss a ride to the city, so he had been going back and forth, too.

"I like the commuting," he said happily.

Then, impulsively, Adam had said, "Junius, this would be a good time to ask Amanda Mouse to visit us. She can come back with you."

Junius wasn't sure. "You know how she feels about the country."

Yes, Adam remembered her very words: ". . . the thought of the country scares me . . . so lonely and so wild."

But she had once said she would come.

So Adam gave Junius a note to take to Amanda.

Dear Amanda,
This is a good time to come to the country. The sky is very blue and the grass is very green.

Your pen friend,
Adam Mouse

P.S. Don't be afraid, Amanda.

Now Adam nibbled on a fat little parsnip and wondered. What would Amanda do?

Why was the truck taking so long? Could a truck lose its way? Just as Adam was pondering this idea, he heard the rumbling of the truck as it pulled into the driveway.

Adam ran as close as he safely could to the edge of the driveway and waited in the grass.

When the farmer had climbed out of the truck and walked to the house, Adam saw Junius jump from the truck.

Adam held his breath.

There she was, right behind Junius.

"Hello, Amanda," said Adam. "Welcome to the country."

Amanda looked puzzled and began sniffing.

"Adam," she said, "what's that strange smell?"

Adam smiled. "That's fresh air, Amanda."

CHAPTER 2

"You came just in time," said Adam.

"In time for what?" Amanda wanted to know.

"For something special," Adam told her. "Let's go this way."

Junius and Amanda followed Adam through the tall grass to a stand of trees.

"This is a good place from which to watch," said Adam. "Look up there, Amanda, at the branch of that tree."

"The wrens!" cried Junius. "That's always a good show."

"What are wrens?" asked Amanda. "What's that on the tree?"

"See that little brown bird over there on the bush?" Adam pointed to a tall leafy bush not far from the tree. "That's a mother wren. And in that nest on the tree are her three little wrens. She's going to show them how to fly."

As they watched, the mother wren flew from the bush to the nest. Then, chirping loudly, she flew back to the bush.

"Here they come!" said Junius. "First flight!"

One of the baby birds rose in the nest, perched for a moment on the edge of the nest, and then took off after his mother. He fluttered a bit, then landed safely on the bush.

"Oh," said Amanda. "I bet she would hug him if she could!"

Once more the mother wren flew from the bush to the nest and back. Once more a baby bird perched on the nest and quickly followed her to the bush.

"Look! She's doing it again," said Amanda. She watched with delight as the mother wren once more flew to the nest, chirping, and then flew back to the bush.

"Here comes the last one," said Adam.

This little wren also came to the edge of the nest and perched there. But he did not follow his mother. The little wren did not move.

"What's the matter?" asked Amanda.

"This one doesn't seem so crazy about flying," said Junius.

Adam said softly,

> *"The baby wren*
> *stands*
> *in the nest.*
>
> *Time to go.*
>
> *But the world seems only*
> *sky above and*
> *earth below.*
>
> *Clinging to the nest's*
> *soft side,*
> *feeling small,*
> *until he dares*
> *he cannot know*
>
> *that he has wings and*
> *will not fall."*

"Where's the mother?" Amanda asked anxiously. "Can't she see he's afraid?"

In a few moments the mother wren returned to the nest. This time she was carrying some food in her mouth. As she approached the nest, the little wren chirped happily. But the mother wren did not drop the food into his eager mouth. Instead, she flew back to the bush.

"The poor little wren!" cried Amanda. "He's so scared and now she won't even feed him!"

Adam smiled. "Just watch."

The little wren chirped again from the nest. The mother flew toward him once more, with food in her mouth. Again she flew back to the bush with the food.

Suddenly the little bird fluttered his new wings and took off after his mother. When he landed on the bush, she fed him.

"Hooray!" cried Amanda. "He made it! Adam, I think he heard your poem."

"I think he was hungry," said Junius. "By the way, so am I."

"So am I," said Adam. "Let's have a picnic in the garden."

"You mean eat out in the open?" said Amanda, wide-eyed. "Like people do in the park?"

"Even better!" said Adam.

CHAPTER 3

Adam Mouse had always been pleased with the way the farmer had laid out his farm. Very nicely planned, thought Adam, with room for all of us.

The garden, which to Adam was a favorite place, stood well apart from the barn and the cornfield, and was a comfortable distance from the farmer's house.

Now as the three friends hurried to the garden, Junius saw the farmer's wife climbing into the truck.

"Look!" he cried. "She's carrying her shopping bag! She's going to the village store. That's where they throw away that wonderful old cheese! I think I'll hop a ride with her."

Before Adam or Amanda could say a word, Junius had raced to the truck and jumped in.

Adam frowned. "Amanda, do you think Junius likes to live dangerously?"

"Don't worry, Adam," said Amanda. "Whenever he comes to the city, he and his friend Orlando Mouse are always on the go."

Adam said nothing, but he was troubled. It seemed to him that Junius was growing more and more restless.

As they went on again to the garden, Amanda said, "Adam, I didn't know there was so much grass in the *whole world*! I like walking on it. The earth is so soft it makes me feel like dancing." She spun around and did a little dance step.

"Ouch!" she cried. "I hit a rock!"

"I'm sorry," said the rock. "Did I hurt you?"

"Turtle!" cried Adam. "It's you! Amanda, this is my very good friend Turtle."

Astonished at Adam's strange-looking friend, Amanda said politely, "How do you do."

"And, Turtle, this is my pen friend, Amanda Mouse."

"Very pleased to meet you," said Turtle in a soft slow voice.

"Turtle, we are on our way to picnic in the garden. Would you care to join us?"

"Thank you, Adam," said Turtle. "I've just come from the garden. I'm full of berries and bugs and I'm on my way back to the pond."

"I want to show Amanda our pond," said Adam, "so we'll see you later."

They watched as Turtle lumbered off.

"He's very poky, isn't he?" Amanda whispered to Adam.

"He's a good friend," Adam told her. "He once gave me a ride to the pond on his back."

"Really? What was it like?"

"I don't know," said Adam. "I fell asleep."

Adam had been wondering how Amanda

would feel when she saw the scarecrow in the garden.

He remembered how alarmed he had been when the farmer first put up the straw man. With that bright red scarf around his neck and that wide-brimmed hat on his head, he had looked quite menacing. Adam had feared that now the Enemy stood right in the middle of the garden.

Then one surprising day, in a reckless moment, Adam had dared to climb the scarecrow and for an amazing time had seen the world from the scarecrow's shirt pocket. After that adventure, Adam had never again been afraid of the scarecrow.

Adam had meant to explain the scarecrow to Amanda, but when they reached the fence that surrounded the garden and were about to slip under it, Amanda stopped short and cried out, "Adam! Be careful! There's someone very strange over there!"

"It's just a scarecrow," Adam said hastily. "Only a make-believe man filled with straw."

"A scarecrow!" said Amanda in amazement. "Are you sure we're safe? He looks as if he's mad at us."

"I think he's sad rather than mad," said Adam.

"*It's garden gossip*
all day
long

16

cricket chatter
bee buzz babble

loud
bird song.

I look
fierce
but, ah, they
know.

I stand
tall
but they all
know.

I'm only
straw.
Can't scare a
crow."

"Oh, Adam," said Amanda. "It's such a comfort to have a friend who's a poet."

It was then that Adam had an idea.

CHAPTER 4

"Do you remember, Amanda," asked Adam, "what happened when I came to see you in the city?"

"Of course," said Amanda. "We went to the library and you discovered that you were a poet!"

"Yes, that was exciting, but I was thinking of something else . . . of your birthday party when I told your friends that I had climbed the scarecrow and they made me an honorary member of your Regional Mountain Climbing Club?"

"You deserved it, Adam," Amanda said warmly. "That was a daring thing to do!"

Adam took a deep breath. "Amanda, how would you like to climb the scarecrow with me? Right now!"

Amanda looked at Adam as if he had invited her to take a trip to the moon.

"Just think!" he urged. "Wouldn't the climbing club be proud of you?"

"Well . . . yes," said Amanda slowly. "But, Adam, what a scary idea!"

"You're an experienced climber, Amanda. All you have to do is stay right behind me and move fast, and you don't look up or down until we reach the pocket of the scarecrow's shirt. It's worth the climb to see the view!"

Amanda stood there, frowning.

What was she thinking, Adam wondered. Maybe it *was* too scary. . . . Maybe. . .

"It's crazy," said Amanda. "Okay. Let's do it."

Amanda said later that she had never moved faster in her life. She and Adam scampered through the garden to the scarecrow at top speed. Adam was right. It was best not to look up or down, just to keep climbing. Amanda felt the pounding of her heart as they reached the scarecrow's shirt pocket and dived in.

After a moment, Adam peered out of the pocket.

"Come and look," he said.

Amanda, looking out, felt as if her eyes had filled with sky.

It was a bright blue afternoon sky, and the wind was playing with the fleecy white clouds.

"The wind is making cloud pictures," said Adam. "I see a cloud fish swimming in the sky!"

Amanda was delighted. "And I see cloud popcorn popping!"

"Look! There's a big vanilla ice-cream cone," said Adam. "It must be delicious. The wind's licking it away."

A tall cloud ship appeared, sailing before the wind into cloud waves.

Suddenly there was a great whiskered face in the sky. Amanda, trembling in spite of herself, cried out, "Adam! A cat!"

Quietly, they watched the welcome wind erase the cat face from the sky.

Then Adam said slowly, "Amanda, there is a real cat on the farm. A cat called Arabella."

21

"I wondered," said Amanda. "But there are so many birds here. They seem to be chirping and twittering and thrumming all over the place."

"That's because the farmer's wife loves the birds. She put a collar of bells on the cat. Now they can all hear the bells of Arabella when she's near." Adam smiled. "And so can we."

"What a wonderful woman!" said Amanda.

Looking down from the scarecrow's pocket, Adam and Amanda had a good view of the garden.

"How green everything is!" Amanda marveled. "Imagine! It all starts here and ends up at the Farmer's Market near my home!"

"It really all starts with seeds," said Adam.

Amanda looked puzzled. "I don't see any seeds."

Adam explained:

"The farmer tucks his tiny seeds
into the earth and waits, and weeds.

Takes his hoe and weeds.

Longs for
rain
and hopes for
sun,
longs for
sun
and hopes for
rain
and
waits and weeds.

Then one day there's
something green,
the promise of a pea or bean,
that seems to say,
'Whew! We've come miles!'

Then at last the farmer smiles."

"And now," said Adam. "Let's have our special picnic."

"Good," said Amanda. "I'm famished. What's so special about it?"

"It's a tasting picnic. We browse through the garden, tasting as we go!"

"Wow!" said Amanda.

CHAPTER 5

The garden was cool and fragrant. Amanda sniffed, took a deep breath and decided, yes, she could really smell the green.

She kept being surprised at the different ways things were growing all around her. She lifted a leaf on a vine—and there was a new little cucumber. She bit into a pod hanging low on a stalk—and out popped a firm fat pea. One dark green plant was so tasty she asked Adam what it was.

"Broccoli," he told her.

"Broccoli!" Amanda could hardly believe it. "But I don't *like* broccoli! . . . Well . . ." She reached for another broccoli leaf and chewed it vigorously. A tasting picnic was certainly an interesting way to eat.

The pumpkin patch was still glowing with large golden flowers that would all soon be pumpkins, and many plump pumpkins had already begun to form.

Suddenly someone called, "Hello, Adam!"

The voice came from inside a young pumpkin, and Amanda jumped back in alarm. Did pumpkins *talk*?

A moment later a mouse peeped out from the little tunnel she had been making in the pumpkin.

"Why, hello, Bessie Mouse," said Adam. "How are you? This is my friend Amanda. She's come from the city for a visit."

Bessie was a bright-eyed motherly little mouse and she looked at Amanda with great interest.

"All the way from the city!" she said. "How wise you are to travel when you're young. I always wanted to travel. Once I even crossed the road to the next farm! But the children came along too soon." She smiled a little sadly. "And here I am trying to gather enough seeds for them right now."

Adam and Amanda offered to help, and soon there was a heap of pumpkin seeds. Together, they brought most of the seeds to the storage tunnel Bessie Mouse had dug right outside the garden fence.

"Help yourself to the rest," Bessie said generously. "I must run now. I'm so glad to have met you, Amanda." And she scampered away.

The pumpkin seeds were delicious. As Amanda and Adam sat eating them (it was very hard to stop), Amanda said thoughtfully, "It's not quite so lonely here as I thought it would be."

"No," said Adam with a deep sigh. "Here comes Chipmunk."

Chipmunk was plainly pleased to see them.

"Ah, there you are, Adam! I see your friend arrived safely from the city. How do you do, ma'am?"

Adam introduced them, and Chipmunk turned eagerly to Amanda.

"My good friend Squirrel once went to the city," he told her. "He got into a car by mistake, and they drove away with him."

He shook his head sorrowfully. "He never came back."

Adam squirmed. He had heard this story many times.

"He's a fine-looking gray squirrel with a nice thick tail," Chipmunk went on. He looked hopefully at Amanda.

"I was wondering . . . if you see him, would you give him a message?"

Amanda looked startled. Then she said, "Of course, Chipmunk. If I see your friend Squirrel, I will be happy to give him a message. Shall I tell him you miss him?"

"Oh, that would be perfect!" Chipmunk's cheek pouches quivered with pleasure. "Yes. Tell him I miss him . . . and that I wish he'd come back home."

Adam felt glad Amanda had not tried to explain that city parks were full of fine-looking gray squirrels with nice thick tails.

Adam and Amanda were still in the garden when they heard the truck in the driveway. They would have known that Junius was back even if they had not seen him. He was preceded by the powerful smell of moldy cheese.

"What a haul!" Junius cried, sniffing the cheese joyfully. "I can't figure out why they throw it away."

The cheese made a perfect dessert for a tasting picnic. As they nibbled, Amanda told Junius how she had climbed the scarecrow.

Junius seemed embarrassed. "Adam hasn't been able to get me up there," he confessed. "I'm afraid of high places."

"Junius, what took you so long getting back?" asked Adam.

"They had to fix a flat tire on our truck," said Junius.

Our truck? Why, he's in love with that truck, thought Adam. An old fear began to grow in his mind.

"And I was beginning to worry," Junius went on, "about getting the corn to the city this evening."

Adam jumped up. Amanda's day in the country was passing too quickly.

"Let's show Amanda the running brook and the pond," said Adam. "We can have a really relaxing time."

A really relaxing time was the last thing it turned out to be.

CHAPTER 6

The way to the pond ran through the
meadow. The meadow had just recently
been cut for hay, and a pungent leftover
smell of cut grass lay gently over everything.

As they ran along the meadow path,
Amanda was thinking how pleasant it was
to breathe this strange air. Junius was deep
in thought about cheese, and Adam was
wondering about Junius.

They all stopped suddenly at the same
moment.

An animal stood in the path directly

ahead of them, digging in the earth, a black-furred animal with a wide white stripe down his back.

"Who's *that*?" Amanda whispered.

"That's Young Skunk," Adam said softly.

"I know about *him*," said Junius. "They say he's trigger happy."

"Is he dangerous?" Amanda asked in alarm.

"Well," said Junius. "A skunk is not an animal you want getting mad at you. He has a powerful spray that he shoots from under his tail. If Young Skunk got angry at us, no one would want to come near us for a long time!"

"Oh, no!" said Amanda. "How awful!"

"We'd never get back in the truck," Junius added gloomily.

"He only shoots at enemies," said Adam. "We're not his enemies. Junius, you and Amanda wait here. I'll be right back."

"Oh, Adam, don't go!" said Amanda. "What if . . . ?"

But Adam was already walking slowly toward the skunk.

Keeping a respectful distance, Adam called, "Hello, Young Skunk. Remember me?"

The skunk looked up from his digging and frowned. Then he looked down at Adam and said, "Who are you?"

"I'm Adam Mouse. We met once before."

"Oh. You're the one they call the Poet Mouse."

"Yes," said Adam shyly.

"They say you make up all kinds of . . . what do they call them?"

"Poems," said Adam.

"Did you ever make up a poem about a skunk?"

"Not yet," said Adam truthfully.

"Can you do it?" Young Skunk asked eagerly. "Can you make up a poem about me?"

"I can try," said Adam. "But you understand, it might be a little rough. Not quite perfect."

"Go ahead," the skunk urged. "Try!"

Adam, in a somewhat unsteady voice, said:

"Skunk
doesn't slink
but walks the earth
with a sense of
worth

and wears with
pride
the bright white
stripe
on his inky
fur.

Skunk won't shrink
to face a
foe.
Gives fair warning
'Better go!'
and many a foe
has slunk
away.

Skunk is
spunky,
mild as well,
and what a tale his
tail
could tell!"

"Why, that's beautiful!" said Young Skunk. "And so true!"

"It needs a little work," said Adam modestly.

"Say it again," said the skunk, "about being spunky and the bright stripe and the tail . . ."

Adam, in a calmer voice, repeated the poem.

"That's wonderful, Poet Mouse," said the skunk. "I can't wait to tell them at home that you made a poem just for me!"

He trotted off to his burrow, repeating happily, "Skunk is spunky . . . skunk won't shrink. . . ."

Adam ran back to Amanda and Junius.

Junius looked at Adam fondly. "What did you do?"

"What did you say?" asked Amanda.

"He wanted a poem," said Adam. "So I told him a poem." He shook his head. "It wasn't one of my best."

Somehow Adam Mouse was not surprised when Junius remarked, in a too casual voice, "I think that while you show Amanda the brook and the pond, I'd like to see what's going on in the cornfield."

What's going on in the cornfield? Surely, thought Adam, Junius knew by now that the farmer was busy breaking off the ripe ears of corn, putting them, still in their husks, into big burlap bags, and that later they would watch as the bags were loaded onto the truck.

"Is there something that worries you about this trip to the city?" Adam asked gently.

"Oh, no," Junius said quickly. "It's just that . . ." He stopped abruptly. "Let's talk about it later."

And he was gone.

CHAPTER 7

The meadow led down to the edge of the woods, and between the woods and the meadow, a brook gurgled cheerfully. The brook ran past the pond, and the pond often overflowed conveniently into the brook.

Adam was trying to explain this to Amanda on their way to the pond. But Amanda was listening to all the sounds in the meadow.

"It's not as quiet here as I thought it would be," she said.

On this late summer afternoon the meadow was bright with clover, and loud with the buzz of bees and the hum and chirp of busy bugs. From somewhere in the meadow a bird kept shrilling, to be answered each time by a shrilling in the distance.

"Those birds have a lot to say to each other," said Adam.

Amanda laughed. "I bet she's telling him to hurry home before supper gets cold!"

The sky was cloudless now, and of a blue that dazzled Amanda. She could not get used to so much open sky, and she kept looking up.

Squinting, she watched a bird with great black wings swooping gracefully overhead.

"Look up there, Adam," she pointed. "Doesn't that look like a plane doing stunts?"

Adam looked up and froze in horror.

The Enemy with Needle Eyes!

"Amanda!" he cried. "Quick! Follow me! And run, run, run!"

Run they did, into the nearest clump of tall weeds.

"Don't move!" said Adam, panting. "That's a hawk!" A hawk, thought Amanda, not an airplane doing stunts!

They stood among the weeds, not daring

to move, watching the sky. They trembled when the hawk soared and dived, and held their breaths till he soared again. After a while, the great bird flew higher and higher until they could no longer see him.

They crept slowly out of the weed clump.

"He's gone now," said Adam. "Are you all right, Amanda?"

"Yes," Amanda said with a sigh. City or country, if you were small in a world full of bigger creatures, the Enemy could be anywhere.

They heard the brook before they saw it, a sound like the soft rushing of wind. The water was sparkling with sunlight and seemed to be running for sheer joy.

Amanda and Adam stood on the bank and watched.

"What a hurry the brook is in!" said Amanda. "And it almost seems to be talking to us."

"Well," said Adam. "It's come a long way and has a lot to tell."

"What is it saying, Adam?" Amanda smiled. "You know, don't you?"

Adam smiled back. "I think it's saying a poem."

"*From the far*
hills
to the faraway
sea
I go.

I flow around
rocks
slip over
stones
and talk to
raindrops.

I carry splinters
of sunlight
and the shadows of
clouds.

Minnows and
sunfish
ride with
me.

Frogs
sit greenly
beside me.

I chatter with
deer,
but I can't stay.
I'm on my way—
on my way
to the
sea."

Amanda took a small leaf from the bank and stuck a small twig into it.

"Here's my boat," she said. "Take it, brook, to the sea."

CHAPTER 8

Amanda had been wondering about the pond. Would it be bigger than a puddle? Bigger than a big puddle?

When she and Adam came at last to the pond, she was not prepared for what she saw.

The pond lay like a great mirror to the sky, and the weeds and reeds and wildflowers that grew around the pond seemed to be growing upside down in the water.

"No wonder you like to come here," said Amanda.

"It's really a very mysterious place," said Adam.

"Does anyone live in the pond?" Amanda asked.

"Yes, indeed!" It was Turtle who answered as he came swimming out of the pond with strong strokes. He climbed slowly onto the bank, and settled himself beside Adam and Amanda.

"This is a busy and crowded place," he said. "Full of bugs and beetles and fish and frogs and little tadpoles that are going to be frogs."

"Look over there, Amanda!" said Adam.

A bug with four long thin legs was moving quickly on the pond like a skater.

Amanda watched in astonishment.

"That bug . . . Adam, is he *walking* on the water?"

Turtle gave a deep chuckle. "He's a water strider, all right. Has feathery feet that don't get wet."

"Walking on water!" Amanda marveled. "What fun that must be!"

Adam turned to Turtle. "Did your baby turtles make it safely to the pond?" he asked.

"Yes, Adam," said Turtle happily. "They all got here."

"Where were they?" asked Amanda, puzzled.

"Well," said Adam. "The mother turtle lays her eggs on the land. When the baby turtles hatch out of the eggs, guess what they do?"

Amanda shook her head. It was extremely difficult to guess what newly hatched turtles would do.

"They head right for the water, don't they, Turtle? Right for the pond!"

"But if they've never seen the pond before," said Amanda, "how do they know where it is?"

"They just know," said Turtle, sounding like a proud papa.

Adam is right, thought Amanda. This is a mysterious place!

Amanda was never quite sure how it happened. It seemed that one moment she was sitting comfortably on a sturdy leaf, peering into the water at the bright orange goldfish swimming by. The next instant a strong breeze had lifted the leaf, slid it into the water, and Amanda found herself drifting on the leaf toward the middle of the pond.

For a moment, Adam, seeing Amanda

adrift, could not move. But this was not the
time to give way to fear.

"Turtle!" he cried.

Turtle, turning his head slowly, saw
what was happening.

"Hop onto my back, Adam," he said,
"and hold fast!"

He started swimming with his long slow
stroke.

"Please, could you hurry a little, Turtle?" said Adam as he saw the leaf drifting
faster.

"We'll make it, Adam," said Turtle.

Very soon, Turtle did come close to the
leaf on which Amanda sat. But the leaf
began to spin away.

"A little more to the right, Turtle," Adam called.

Turtle moved to the right, but the leaf was still out of reach.

Adam's heart was pounding. "Turn left now!" he cried.

Turtle moved left, stretched his head, and caught the leaf in his mouth.

"Amanda." Adam tried to sound calm, but his voice was suddenly squeaky. "Reach up to me. Closer, Turtle, please! . . . *Now, Amanda!*" And with Adam's help, Amanda leaped safely onto Turtle's back.

Steadily and very carefully, Turtle swam back to the shore. He clambered onto the bank where Adam and Amanda jumped down from his back.

"Thank you, dear Turtle!" exclaimed Amanda.

"What a friend you are!" said Adam. There was much more he wished he could say.

"My pleasure," said Turtle. "Are you both all right now?"

Amanda and Adam looked at each other. It was hard to talk. They nodded.

"Then good-bye for now," said Turtle, and he slipped back into the pond.

Adam did not tell Amanda what had happened to the leaf. He hoped she hadn't noticed.

Amanda did not tell Adam that she had seen the leaf drift out of the pond into the running brook—on the way to the sea.

CHAPTER 9

"Don't be upset, Adam," said Amanda.

They were making their way back through the meadow. It was dusk, and the light was slowly fading from the sky. Time to meet Junius at the truck.

"But weren't you scared, Amanda?" asked Adam.

"Of course I was. It all happened so fast! But as soon as I saw you and Turtle, I knew I'd be safe."

I wish *I* had been so sure, thought Adam.

"Anyway," said Amanda. "We live with narrow escapes, don't we, Adam?"

Adam sighed. It was true. "But I wanted

you to have a good time in the country."

"Adam," said Amanda fervently, "I've had one of the most interesting times of my life!"

"Really?" Adam began to feel better.

It was pleasant walking through the meadow in the light of day on its way to evening. A pale white moon appeared in the sky, as if it could not wait for the dark.

Suddenly Amanda stopped.

"What's going on out there?" she asked.

Lights were flickering on and off in the meadow. Bright dots of light. Flashing on and off.

"Who's turning on all those lights?" she wanted to know.

"Bugs," said Adam.

"Bugs!"

"Yes. Fireflies. They make that light with their own bodies," said Adam.

> *"Fireflies*
> *Flash*
> *Their cold gold glow*
> *Upon the*
> *Night.*

Flickering,
Seeking.

Speaking
the language of
Light,
They find one
Another."

"Is *that* what they're doing?" Amanda shook her head in wonderment. "Bugs that walk on water! Bugs that make lights! I'm not sure that anyone back home will believe me!"

Junius greeted them eagerly.

"The farmer's almost finished loading," he told them. "As soon as he gets into the truck to go, we jump on and make for the hay hill."

To Amanda's surprise, Bessie Mouse and Chipmunk were also there in the tall grass by the driveway.

"We came to see you off," said Bessie Mouse. "Here are some pumpkin seeds for your trip. My, I wish I were going to the city!"

"What yummy seeds! Thanks, Bessie Mouse. Maybe someday you will go!"

"To the city?" cried Chipmunk. "Too dangerous! But if I were going, I'd take along a nice chestnut, like this." And he gave Amanda a plump peeled chestnut.

"Why, thank you, Chipmunk," said Amanda. "I've never had one before."

Meanwhile, Junius had taken Adam aside.

"Adam," he said. "I've been wanting to tell you that . . . that . . . I'd . . . well . . . that I'd like to stay in the city for a while . . . with Orlando Mouse . . . not come right back, I mean."

"I know," said Adam.

"You *know*?" Junius was startled.

"Every once in a while, Junius, you need some real excitement . . . and some pepperoni pizza."

"Orlando has found a new Italian restaurant," said Junius, smacking his lips. "He says the spaghetti sauce is terrific!"

"And you need the jazz, too, Junius . . . something to dance to."

"We *are* different, aren't we?" said Junius. "I guess there's a kind of excitement being a poet that I'll never know."

"Best friends are often different," said Adam. "Maybe that's good. I'd never have gotten to the city without you!"

"And I'd never really see what I'm looking at without your poems." They smiled at each other. "Well, I'll be back soon after the last load of corn gets delivered next week. With a letter, as usual, from your pen friend, Amanda!"

The truck was loaded.

It was time to go.

"Adam," said Amanda. "I'm taking back a lot of country. Everything at the Farmer's Market will taste better, now that I've seen how things grow."

"Even broccoli?" said Adam with a smile.

"Even broccoli! I'm taking back other things, too, like the sound of that brook running, and the feel of all that grass."

Adam handed Amanda a small envelope. "Here's something for you to read on your way home."

Amanda could feel the rustle of paper inside the envelope.

"I hope it's a poem!" she said. Then she saw what was written on the envelope: FOR AMANDA WHO WAS NOT AFRAID.

"Thank you, Adam," she said. "I wouldn't have missed this day!"

Adam watched as Junius and Amanda jumped into the truck, and he waited in the tall grass until the truck had pulled away.

He stood there, thinking—remembering all that he had brought back from his own adventurous trip to the city, and reliving the happenings of this special day.

He might have stayed there, deep in thought. But suddenly he heard it—the sound of bells. The bells of Arabella!

In an instant he had scampered into a tunnel in the grass and was gone.